SANDI PATTI

LE VOYAGE

with
MATT BAUGHER

Based on an Original Concept by
BOB FARRELL • GREG NELSON

WORD PUBLISHING

Dallas • London • Vancouver • Melbourne

LE VOYAGE by Sandi Patti. Copyright © 1993 by Word Publishing. All rights reserved. No part of this publication may be reproduced, stored in a retrieval system, or transmitted in any form or by any means—electronic, mechanical, photocopy, recording, or any other—except for brief quotations in printed reviews, without the prior permission of the publisher.

Song lyrics by Bob Farrell and Greg Nelson © 1993 Gentle Ben Music (adm. by Word, Inc.)/Dayspring Music (a div. of Word, Inc.)/BMI/Summerdawn Music/Steadfast Music (adm. by Copyright Management Inc.)/ASCAP.

Library of Congress Cataloging-in-Publication Data

Patti, Sandi, 1956–
    Le voyage / Sandi Patti.
      p.   cm.
    ISBN 0–8499–1065–X
    I. Title.
  PS3566.A82484L4   1993
  813'.54—dc20   93–7191
                                               CIP

3 4 5 6 9 BMG 9 8 7 6 5 4 3 2 1
Printed in the United States of America.

This book is lovingly dedicated to, and in honor of, my beloved Companion, Jesus Christ, who has never stopped loving me, believing in me, picking me up when I fall, and giving me the strength to journey on.

And take the hand of the one who'll be my Companion
For He will show me the place to begin . . .

from "Little Narrow Gate"

Acknowledgments and Thanks

I must thank some wonderful friends who have made my journey sweeter and richer:

Greg Nelson—My friend and producer (in that order) who came to me with the original concept of *Le Voyage* that began a journey for me that I will never forget.

Bob Farrell—A poet's poet, who along with Greg Nelson birthed *Le Voyage* and allowed me to help bring this project to maturation.

Matt Baugher—A dear and loyal friend and comrade who contributed equally to the writing of this book with me. I thank you, Matt, for everything.

My Word Family—Who never stopped believing in me and have never withdrawn their love from me, even though I may have made these last couple of years tough for them. You are so appreciated.

With the wind at my back . . . the journey before me
I set my feet on the road that leads to life.

from "Little Narrow Gate"

I

*I*N A PLACE NOT FAR from here, in a time close to our own, a baby girl was born. She came from a long line of Seekers of Truth, and she was given the name Traveler. Traveler lived and grew, pretty much as little girls do, until the day it was time for her to set out on her journey of life.

There was, in fact, a party in Traveler's honor that day. In the midst of the festivities, her father called Traveler into his study.

"Well, my dear, you'll be going out on your own now," he began somewhat stiffly. "I trust you'll take everything your mother and I have said to heart. We want very much for you to follow in our footsteps."

"Why yes, Father," the young Traveler answered, for she had no reason to believe that her journey would lead anywhere other than where it was expected to, wherever that was.

"Good girl," he murmured. He reached into his desk drawer and with a great show of ceremony, drew out an antique brass compass. It was large, about six inches across, and gleamed in the firelight. "This compass belonged to your grandmother and her father before her. She gave it to me many years ago. See that you take good care of it, use it in your journey, and above all, preserve it for future generations. This is the way of our family, Seekers of Truth."

Traveler took the compass from her father's hand. Brass knobs outlined the circumference. It was ornate and heavier than it looked. "This compass will just cause extra weight in my pack," she thought. Immediately she chastised herself for feeling ungrateful. Her wise father seemed to trust it and it would surely be worth the extra weight to have a guide to point her way.

The very next day Traveler readied her pack and set out on her journey. She left her father's house and started down a trail called Familiar. She passed all the familiar landmarks of her youth—the building in which she had been schooled, her grandmother's cottage, the little church where she sat and tried to stay awake each Sunday. By

Sandi Patti

dusk that very first day, she came to a crossroads. Familiar Trail ended. Already, she must make a choice.

Traveler took her compass from her pack, squinted up at the sky, looked down at the compass, and blithely chose the road to the left marked New Beginnings, saying to herself, "I don't know where this journey will lead. I don't know where I'm going. But this *is* an adventure."

Soon Traveler came to a roadside inn on New Beginnings Road. She decided to stop for she was tired and hungry.

As she lay down for the night, the first stirrings of doubt tugged at Traveler's heart. "What if I didn't choose the right road?" she worried. "How will I know? Where will my life lead? Will I do the right thing? Am I even asking the right questions?" She tossed for a time, pondering these things.

Then, as she turned over for what seemed the millionth time, a feeling of peace came over her, like a warm blanket. She heard a small voice that seemed to come from her heart, "Journey and you will find." And Traveler was able to sleep.

Le Voyage

In the morning, Traveler was surprised to find many other travelers getting ready to set out from the inn. They chatted over their breakfast about where they had been and where they were going. From what she overheard, many of them had been on the road far longer than she had.

As she was pondering this new experience, a young man approached Traveler. "Hello, my name is Challenger. I belong to the family of Any Man. You look fresh, as if you haven't been traveling very far or long."

Traveler wasn't at all sure she should talk with this stranger, but remembering her manners she introduced herself. "My name is Traveler."

"But you haven't been traveling long, have you?" Challenger pressed his question.

"No, but why do you ask?" There was something about Challenger that compelled Traveler to answer his question.

"Well, I thought you might like to join my group. We will be leaving soon. We want to journey far today. We have no desire to become one of those," and so saying, he pointed to a group of people lounging in the corner. They sat with their feet up on a table. Some of them read, some of them dozed, some just stared up at the ceiling.

"They look as if they might have been there awhile," Traveler observed.

"They have," Challenger answered. "They're called the Passers-by."

"And why are they called that?"

"They have stopped following their heart's desire. They're not really living. If a traveler doesn't follow the call, then he has ceased to travel," Challenger spat out as if he were angry.

"Well, going back to your question, I do not yet know where I travel. I am seeking to find my way. So I don't know if I should go with you. Where is your group heading?" Traveler was beginning to think Challenger wouldn't be such a bad companion.

"Why, you poor young thing. We're headed for the City of Dreams, of course. You had better come with us," Challenger replied not unkindly.

"Hmm, the City of Dreams. That sounds nice. I wonder if that's where my compass will lead," Traveler replied.

"Compass?" Challenger actually skipped a few steps in his excitement. "What compass do you have?"

"Why the compass handed down from my father and his mother before him. I am from the Seekers of Truth," Traveler responded.

"Then you *must* come with us." Challenger waved his arms, beckoning to his group. "Come over here. Meet Traveler, from the Seekers of Truth. She has one of those compasses we've been hearing about. I've asked her to join us."

The others spoke all at once. "A compass! How wonderful," they chorused. "Join us, please do," one said. "We've wanted to meet someone like you," another added.

So it was settled. Traveler left the inn on New Beginnings Road with Challenger and his group. They traveled together for some time, always striving to find their way. Sometimes they traveled in silence, sometimes in laughter. Sometimes they argued about the meaning of their journey and quite honestly, sometimes the road just seemed long. They were tired and cried in frustration. But they stayed together, because even uncertainty can bring about a sort of camaraderie.

Quite often they met Passers-by in an inn, or even sitting by the side of the road. Seeing these lost souls always spurred them on. "We're not like those people," they said. "Life won't pass us by. We'll keep moving until we find the City of Dreams." One beautiful spring day, Traveler sat lost in thought as they rested along the Road of Uncertainty, puzzling about how little she really knew about her fellow pilgrims.

A cranky shout broke into her reverie, "Let's pick up the pace folks. We've got to get off this road. Have you forgotten the purpose of our trip?"

"No," the others answered as one. Traveler said nothing.

"We must reach the City of Dreams," Challenger exhorted.

"Yes," another answered, "we have only ourselves to rely on."

"So let's get on with it," another chimed in. "We won't get anywhere by hanging around here in the present."

"You're right," Challenger reminded them. "We must always look to tomorrow. For in some tomorrow, we'll find our City of Dreams."

Traveler remained silent. She had heard Challenger say more than once that the present moment was of no consequence. But she had never been able to accept his philosophy. Besides, another question had been nagging at her lately, "Why are we so set on going to the City of Dreams when none of us knows where it is and what we'll find there?"

Nevertheless, she journeyed on with the group. The shadows grew longer and longer on the Road of Uncertainty. The pilgrims began to trip over roots of the Know-Nothing Trees in the growing darkness. The road narrowed and seemed almost to end.

Challenger wasn't any surer than anyone else about where they were. But he aimed to find out. "Traveler," he called out. "We're off course. And it's your fault. The map indicates a fork in the road that we have missed. Your compass led us to this place."

"That's not entirely true," Traveler began to protest.

"Never mind that. Check your wretched compass. It's your job to get us out of here. Does that thing work or not?"

"Well, yes, but . . ." Traveler got no further in her reply.

"I'm waiting. Are you going to continue to let others bear the burden

Sandi Patti

of the success of this journey? Or are you going to tell us where to go?" Challenger was getting angrier.

She was uncertain, but she began to speak. "This appears to be the right way; at least that's what my compass says. But my heart says that if we rest until morning, the map will be clearer, and we will be able to see our way."

"Shirking your responsibility, huh, Traveler?" Challenger was totally disgusted. "Fine, you stay here. The rest of us are going to retrace our steps until we find that fork. We must have missed it."

II

*T*HE GROUP DID INDEED go with Challenger, leaving Traveler sitting by the side of the road. She looked around to see if she were truly alone. It wasn't as if she hadn't made friends along her journey. She had, both in the group she traveled with and with others whose path crossed theirs.

"The trouble is," she thought to herself, "that the others all seem so sure of themselves. They don't have the same questions as I do about where we're going or why we're even on this trip. They just keep going. I feel like I don't have any friends to share my deepest feelings with. And when you can't share your innermost feelings, you don't really have friends."

Having thought that, Traveler jumped up. She couldn't stay here alone. She was already talking to herself. That wouldn't do.

She sank down again, indecisive and confused. "No," she thought, "there must be another journey. I don't want to go to the City of Dreams. There has to be another path to follow."

"There is," a gentle but strong voice rang out.

"Who's there?" Traveler cried. She was pretty sure she hadn't spoken aloud. This was scary. "Who are you?"

"One who has come to say there is another path. I have come to tell you the beckoning in your heart is true. I am called Companion."

"And you say that I will find my way? The others have already left to find the road to the City of Dreams. I too want to find my heart's

Sandi Patti

desire. But I don't think I can catch up with them." Traveler was beginning to feel alone again, despite the friendly voice of her as yet unseen Companion.

Companion spoke reassuringly as he stepped out of the woods. "You can only embark on your own journey. You were right to wonder about the direction. You cannot travel others' paths. They must find their own, and so must you."

"Oh, no," Traveler lamented, "and I've wasted all this time wandering around with Challenger's group. When will my journey begin?"

Companion chuckled. "Oh, my dear, it has already begun. It began the day you left your father's house. That moment, the moment your heart's beckoning became so great that you had to go, that's when your journey began."

"You mean I haven't wasted all this time?" Traveler found that a bit difficult to believe, since here she was lost on the Road of Uncertainty.

"No, little one, you have not. You chose not to follow the others just now. And in doing so, your feet found the Narrow Path. Look closely, Traveler."

Le Voyage

"How do you know my name?" she asked, startled.

"I have always known it. Now look, and tell me what you see."

Traveler squinted down at their feet. "I think my eyes are playing tricks on me. Sometimes I see a path, and then it just disappears."

Companion understood. He had heard this before. "That's perfectly normal in the beginning. Your eyes are becoming new. Be patient. Trust them, and look ahead. What do you see?"

"The path seems to lead up that little hill. I can't quite . . ." Traveler stopped to muse for a minute. "Ah, yes, I see it. There's a very small gate." As she said these words she noticed that dawn had come. She and Companion must have talked the night away. Yet it didn't seem like such a long time.

"Your heart does not deceive you, Traveler. Now tell me, what else do you see?"

"Well, I can't quite *see* it, but my heart seems to tell me that this Little Narrow Gate leads to great things," Traveler replied.

Companion smiled. "Ah, yes," he murmured to himself, "Traveler sees more than she thinks she does."

Sandi Patti

There's a little narrow gate
At the top of a hill
And it beckons my heart to enter in
And follow where it will . . . oh, where it will
And the path that leads through this gate of dreams
Takes me away.
All my life I've been waiting
Could this be the place I can start?

from "Little Narrow Gate"

Traveler hadn't felt this excited even on that very first day when she left her father's house. Something powerful was happening. "But can I trust this?" she said to herself. "After all, the last I knew I was on the Road of Uncertainty. I've been disappointed so many times. And shed so many tears. And Challenger and the others just left me alone. How do I know this one won't as well?"

"Traveler," Companion began gently. "I won't abandon you."

"How do you do that?" Traveler laughed. "You seem to know what I am thinking."

Sandi Patti

"I do," said Companion. "And right now you're wondering whether you should go through the gate. I ask you what you choose. Do you choose to follow the path your heart and eyes see and go through the gate?"

Traveler thought for the briefest of moments. "I do want to go, Companion. I am called. My heart must answer."

With that, she began to run toward the gate. She ran a way before she thought about Companion. Just as she turned to look for him, he appeared at her side.

"Where do you come from, Companion? And where are you going?"

"I come from the Homeplace," he responded. "The place where hearts find their home. As to where I am going, well . . ." "Oh, dear Companion, do come with me," Traveler pleaded, realizing for the first time since the others left that maybe she wouldn't have to journey entirely alone.

"I was hoping you would ask," Companion said, with delight on his face and joy in his heart.

And take the hand of the One who'll be my companion
For He will show me the place to begin.

from "Little Narrow Gate"

And so they went through the gate. First Traveler, and then Companion, who made a point of leaving the gate open. Traveler noticed immediately.

"Shouldn't we close it?" she asked.

"My Father will take care of that."

III

*A*ND SO THEY WENT ON. Traveler couldn't believe the beauty of their surroundings. Everything looked so clean, so fresh. Her heart overflowed. An exhilaration beyond words swept over her. "The sky," she exclaimed, "Companion, do look at the sky. Never before has it been so blue. Look at those trees, how green! Those

Sandi Patti

birds, how they fly together in perfect formation. Why, I'm speech-less."

Companion laughed. "You don't sound speechless, dear little Traveler. Look behind you."

Traveler did. "Oh, Companion," her voice grew hoarse with won-der. "Why, that's where I came from, down in that valley. I can see it from here, the Road of Uncertainty, and New Beginnings Road, and even Familiar Trail. Everything was so murky and overwhelming down there. But up here, how clear the air is." And she turned again. She pointed ahead with her finger. "See how well defined the path is."

> *I can hardly believe my feet have brought me this far*
> *To the top of a mountain, at the edge of the stars*
> *And I know there's a reason God has shown me this place*
> *To see with new vision the journey I face*
> *I'm a river that reels through the distance below*
> *Winding through choices and the way I must go.*
>
> from "The Long Look"

Companion remained quiet for a long time. No matter how many times he'd seen it, there was nothing quite like the feeling he had when someone got her first taste of Long Look Mountain, seeing all of Life's Abundant Joys so clearly. There was the Sky of Beauty, the Warm Sun of Love, and the Harmony of all God's Creatures. He watched and listened in satisfaction as Traveler saw and named all these things and more.

He only spoke to answer her unspoken question. "No, this is not the end, but only the beginning. You must leave this mountain to continue your journey. And once you leave, the things you see now and the feelings you feel now will begin to grow dim unless you make a conscious choice to remember them. Think on these things daily, Traveler. They will help you in times to come."

Traveler heard most of Companion's long speech. But, to be honest, it was hard for her to imagine not remembering this place when she felt so good. "How could I forget something this clear?" she asked herself. And then another thought came to her. She reached into her

Sandi Patti

pack. Yes, it was still there. "If I do get lost on this path, I still have my compass," she thought.

It never occurred to Traveler to wonder why her compass hadn't led her to Long Look Mountain.

> *Every summit I reach seems the highest I've been*
> *With my valleys below God renews me again*
> *I can say my goodbyes to all the struggle and tears*
> *When I see through His eyes I've got nothing to fear*
> *For joy's there to meet me and wisdom's my friend*
> *My companions that help me find purpose again.*
>
> from "The Long Look"

Now Traveler journeyed in earnest. With clear eyes and heart, with strong feet and resolve, she walked, and sometimes ran toward her future. Days passed, some tougher than others, but still she followed the Narrow Path. It was always there. She wasn't sure what compelled her to keep moving. She met other pilgrims, but she refused to join their groups. She explained to them, "I must make my own choices. I wish you a good journey, and I pray that you wish the same for me."

Traveler felt good about the direction of her life. She had met a kind and understanding Companion who seemed to know her like no one ever had before. She certainly would not become a Passer-by. In fact she scarcely saw them anymore.

Then one day, when the sun barely shone through the mist and the Narrow Path was hard to see, once again she began asking questions and analyzing her progress. And she thought, "Where am I? Why is it growing dark? Am I making progress? And if I have a Companion, where is he? I haven't seen him for ages."

Traveler stopped, realizing that she had wandered away from Companion. She was in fact at a crossroads. She checked her trusty compass, but the needle just flopped back and forth. It didn't seem to be working properly. Then she looked up at the sign. "Ah," she said to herself, "maybe I should take that way, the Road of Good Intentions. But where is Companion?"

Sandi Patti

Just then he appeared. He had been right behind her on the path, of course, letting her lead the way.

"Hurry up, Companion," Traveler was feeling irritated. "Why can't you keep up? I don't have all life you know."

Companion just nodded. And Traveler felt even more irritated. "I'm going this way, along the Road of Good Intentions, and you can't stop me," she threatened.

Then she stopped herself. "Why am I so irritated with Companion?" she wondered. "Perhaps I'd better sit down and rest before I veer off the Narrow Path. So much has happened so fast. Yes, that's what I should do."

Unfortunately as she rested, she talked herself into taking the Road of Good Intentions after all. Her reasoning went something like this: "Companion said I must make choices. And I know that I must. So if I have the intention of doing good and of following my heart's true desire, then it stands to reason I should go down the Road of Good Intentions."

Having convinced herself, and without a further thought to Companion, she did just that. Lo and behold, as she walked, the day grew a bit brighter, not sunshiny bright like on Long Look Mountain, but more like an artificial light. But Traveler didn't care. She could see. And so she walked on.

As she walked she became hungry. And just as she became conscious of her hunger she saw a bush by the side of the road. Its bright, red berries beckoned to her. "Eat of me," they seemed to say. "I am here for you." And so she ate.

After she ate, she began to think about the missing Companion. He seemed to have abandoned her. "He's just like all the others," she thought. "He forced me to take the Narrow Path. Then when I left it, he disappeared. Well, I'm just fine without him."

But the berries made her thirsty—*very* thirsty. And, as soon as she noticed her thirst, like magic, she came upon a clear, running stream. She bent, scooped the water in her hands, and drank her fill. But when she'd finished drinking, a vile, sour aftertaste lingered in her mouth.

Sandi Patti

Here she was, alone on the Road of Good Intentions with a sour mouth and the beginnings of a stomachache. Yet could it be? She thought she saw some other pilgrims up ahead. Maybe if she hurried she could catch up with them. Traveler began to run.

She ran for a long time until she realized something strange. The longer she ran, the more the Road of Good Intentions looked just the same. She was running in place.

Finally, out of breath, Traveler stopped running. She knew she needed to find real food and shelter soon. "Think, girl," she said to herself. "What was it I was supposed to remember about Life's Abundant Joys?" In her misery, she called out to Companion, "Why have you let me get into this mess?" Although her voice was angry, her heart remained still.

So many choices about where to go. She'd tried to make the right ones. Going down the Road of Good Intentions by herself had seemed like a good choice. This was just one of many times when she'd decided to do something, confident that it was right, and then it had turned out all wrong. "Oh why, oh why, did I ever leave Companion and the Narrow Path?" she moaned, becoming dizzy.

Her head hurt, her stomach hurt, her feet hurt, but most of all her heart hurt. She was alone. She needed someone to talk to.

"Oh, dear Companion, please come back." Traveler didn't know whether she spoke aloud or not.

"A gentle voice answered, "I am here."

Traveler burst into tears. "Why did you leave me? I am so sick and lost. Where have you been?"

"I did not leave you, and I have been where I always am," came Companion's loving, if enigmatic, reply. "Now tell me what you have been doing and where you hurt."

So Traveler told Companion about eating the berries and drinking from the brook and running and running, but not getting anywhere. Finally in frustration, she ended, crying and talking at the same time, "Up on Long Look Mountain everything seemed so clear. Now I'm lost on some stupid road that doesn't go anywhere with more questions than answers. Oh, Companion, where have I been and where am I going?"

Companion listened to all she said. He listened to her words and to her heart. He couldn't take away her pain and sickness. He couldn't take

Sandi Patti

away her questions. He knew she needed them all. But he could explain a few things to her.

"Listen carefully," he said. "This Road of Good Intentions really doesn't lead anywhere. Those berries you ate are Berries of Deception. And that water you drank, why, that was from the Brook of Doubt. The strong aftertaste makes you doubt yourself."

"Oh, woe is me! I should never have left the Narrow Path." Traveler began to cry even more bitterly. "I'll never find it again. I don't know the way."

"Traveler, my dear, calm yourself," Companion continued. "The pace of your journey is as important as the direction. You just started going a little too fast, and then you made one wrong turn, and that led to another. If you move too fast, you will not understand the depth of your journey. You won't be able to follow the Narrow Path. If you go too slow, of course, you risk stopping altogether and becoming a Passer-by. You must walk with me Traveler, for I know the best pace for you. I will never leave you, but you must stay close to me. I am your Companion."

Le Voyage

Hearing these words, Traveler did indeed begin to feel better, calmer. Still, she was puzzled. "How will I know if I am staying close to you?" she asked. "How do I know I won't get lost again? And how do I know you won't get sick of hearing me cry and complain? Oh, my head hurts when I think of all the questions I have."

"I know you have questions that overwhelm you, Traveler," Companion replied. "Questions are part of your journey. And you must never be afraid to ask them. No question you can ask and nothing you say will make me leave. Was I not happy with you when you discovered Life's Abundant Joys? And am I not with you now when you ate of the Berries of Deception and drank of the Water of Doubt and became sick and hurting? Traveler, look into my eyes and know that I love you."

She looked and saw such love unlike any she had felt before. Companion did not ask her to live as her family had always lived, as her father had. Companion did not demand that she know the way, as Challenger had. She didn't have to do anything, or prove anything, or find anything to earn Companion's love. The kind of love she had felt before seemed like a weight—something she had to earn. She couldn't move at all and she was constantly struggling against that weight. But this was new. This kind of love held her safe and secure. "Why, he wants nothing from me except that I stay with him," she thought. Traveler felt loved unconditionally.

Companion knew her thoughts and her heart. He said, "I am with you in ways you cannot know, in the wind, the trees, the sun, the stars, everywhere. You can stay with me because I will stay with you."

> *My heart goes out to you as you go your way*
> *Take strength, my friend, in all you do*
> *I pray that God will keep you in loving care*
> *And that all the stars shine down on you.*

from "All the Stars"

"You seem to know so much about me, Companion," Traveler said. "Tell me about yourself. I want to know you. Tell me more about Homeplace."

"My Father is there. But I spend much of my time in this world as well."

"And who is your Father? Is he a kind man like you, Companion?"

Companion always loved to answer this question. "My Father and I are very much alike indeed. In fact, some say if you've seen me, you've seen my Father. It is he who sent me to you, Traveler. He heard your heart's cry."

Companion found a nice grassy spot beside the road to sit. "Join me here, Traveler. It is good to rest and talk as good friends should." There were few things that Companion loved more than talking about his Homeplace.

Companion warmed to his subject. "The Homeplace has always been. It is a place of joy and fulfillment, contentment and peace. In the Homeplace, the journey continues but the burdens of this life are stripped away, and you see the truth, clearly and honestly, with no distractions, with no questions. It is a place where you can truly commune with others who have longed for a place to call Home."

Sandi Patti

"It sounds so lovely," Traveler murmured. "But will there be a place for me there?"

Companion smiled "Of course, dear one, for my Father has prepared a place for you. He awaits your coming."

"How will I know when I'm on my way to Homeplace?" she asked.

"You are already on your way," Companion replied. "Remember what I said to you about seeing the Narrow Path with your eyes and your heart. You must just keep doing that and you will reach Home. Or rather Home will find you."

> *It's a land where dreams come true and doubts are swept away*
> *A homeplace to the traveler who's questioning his way*
> *And if you're lost the power of love will bring you home*
>
> *Like the friendship of a family as they gather round a fire*
> *It's the warmth of that acceptance that everyone desires*
> *And if you're cold the homeplace burns with flames of love.*

from "Home Will Find You"

Companion wrapped Traveler warm in his cloak. "Hush now. Rest, for the night is almost gone. When the sun rises we will set out again."

In the morning, with newfound energy, Traveler made her way again. They left the Road of Good Intentions behind, and once more she could see and feel the Narrow Path. Her mind and spirit were renewed, but the going was not always easy. She kept moving, though not too fast, and not too slow.

As Companion and Traveler journeyed they talked. Traveler listened to Companion with fascination. It seemed impossible that anyone could understand things with such knowledge and clarity.

When Traveler would have reached for a Berry of Deception, which appeared again as soon as she was hungry, Companion gently guided her to the Fruit of Truth instead. And when she thirsted, he led her directly to the Well of Wisdom, guiding her away from the Brook of Doubt.

The lesson she learned from the Seeds of Curiosity didn't seem funny when she found the first ones. Traveler spotted a seed and picked it up. Something told her to sit down beside the path, but she

Sandi Patti

didn't, of course. Instead she said to Companion, "I must plant this seed and see what grows."

Companion, as always, let her choose what to do. So she planted the seed and watched as it grew into a tangled vine. It seemed to take only a minute. Each stem went out in a different direction, and Traveler insisted on following several to their ends, trying to gather up all the new seeds. Of course she got tangled in the vines and wasted a lot of time and energy going around in circles. Later on she said, "Curiosity got me all tangled up," and both of them giggled.

The Stones of Strength were perhaps the most intriguing. Traveler encountered the first one late in the day. There it was, where it hadn't been just a minute before, blocking the Narrow Path. First she tried to shove it aside—it wouldn't budge. Then she kicked it, getting nothing but a sore toe for her trouble. Finally, in frustration, she sat down on it, for it had grown into a large boulder. As she sat, the voice in her heart said, "Pick it up and put it in your pack."

"Oh sure," she said aloud, "this stone must weigh half a ton and I'm going to put it in my pack!" But that's exactly what she did. She discovered that by picking up the stones one by one and placing them in her travel pouch, she was beginning to make progress. The stones actually became smaller after she placed them in her pouch. Along the path, Traveler found more and more of these stones.

IV

*T*HEY JOURNEYED ON. Companion, of course, knew everything about Traveler, yet still he delighted as she discovered things about herself and shared them with him. And, at Traveler's request, Companion continued to tell stories about himself and his Father. After a while, Traveler felt as if she had known Companion her whole life. "What did I ever do without you?" she asked him one day as they were sitting at rest.

"Oh, I was never far from you," Companion answered. "Remember when you used to sit in that small church every Sunday with your grandmother?"

"You were there?" Traveler asked. "I never saw you."

"Your heart wasn't beckoning you yet, that's why. And in your school, and in your girlhood home, I was there too. Remember, I am never far away."

"Well, I'm glad that I know you're here now," sighed Traveler. "And I'd love to sit here forever, but I think we must be on our way."

"Whatever you choose," replied Companion, smiling at her.

So they walked along on the Narrow Path and beside the River of Innocence. Traveler found comfort in hearing the lovely stream burble. Daily she washed her hands and face in it and drank of its sweet water. But one morning, after a particularly restless night worrying that she might not be going in the right direction, she awoke to silence.

At first she didn't know what was wrong. Then, hearing only the silence, missing the reassuring sound of the River of Innocence, she panicked. "Companion," she jumped up. "Companion, where are you? The river—it's gone."

More silence. No answer. "Oh no," wailed Traveler. I knew I took a wrong turn yesterday. Now Companion is gone, and I've lost the Narrow Path."

Some time passed as she sat there wringing her hands and moaning. Then she became still. And as she quieted herself she heard that loving voice once again.

"My dear girl, why do you worry? You have not lost your way. When you take a wrong turn, remember all you have to do is know that I will always be with you. Now hush; do you hear the river?"

And so she did. She had not lost the River of Innocence or the Narrow Path after all. She only needed to quiet herself and let her heart call out to them.

That day they walked long. The Narrow Path grew steep. Despite Companion's reassurance, Traveler grew tired. Her doubts had taken much energy from her. She was lonely too for the camaraderie of other pilgrims.

"If only I could stop for a while, rest, talk with . . ." Wait! Was that singing she heard? She hadn't realized how long it had been since she'd heard a voice other than her own or that of her trusted companion. And that bright haze on the horizon. Those were lights, not the moon. Someone else was on the path, quite nearby it seemed.

Sandi Patti

Traveler's laughter rang out, startling an owl from a nearby tree. "Companion! Companion!" she cried out. "Is it true? Are there others near here? Is there a place to stop?"

Companion had been expecting this. "It is the City of Rest, Traveler. A much needed respite to be sure, but you must be careful."

"Careful? Of what?" Traveler was getting annoyed with Companion again. Here they were near others for the first time in who knew how long and he was telling her to be careful.

"Of yourself," Companion replied patiently. "You must rest, yes, that is crucial to continuing your journey. But you must guard against complacency and false security."

"Oh, Companion, you worry too much," Traveler laughed.

"No, my dear, I do not," Companion replied. For truly he did not worry. Yet he did have Traveler's best interests at heart, which is why he reminded her, "Remember the Berries of Deception and the Brook of Doubt. Things are not always what they seem. They can breed discontent, make you doubt, throw you off your true course."

But Traveler wasn't listening. In fact, at this moment she was sprinting full tilt down the hill toward the entrance to the City of Rest.

V

$\mathcal{A}$ GATEKEEPER GREETED HER with a smile. "Welcome, welcome to the City of Rest on the path where all becomes clear." Traveler did not notice that his eyes and heart were not smiling too.

She stepped through the gate and stopped to look around. She saw a lovely small city with many people sitting on benches, stopping to chat in small groups, lolling against buildings. No one seemed to be going anywhere in much of a hurry. As soon as she stopped, she began to shiver in the chill night air.

"Hello," she called to a friendly young man leaning against a portal to the gate. "Are you also travelers?"

"We prefer to be called Voluntary Passengers," he answered. "We go with the flow. Actual traveling requires so much strength, especially if you carry your own burden."

Sandi Patti

"But you had to travel to get to this place, did you not?" Traveler was confused.

"Of course. However, we have been resting for many years now. It's enjoyable here. Who's to say the Homeplace is any better? No one's ever been there. Perhaps someday I'll go with the others when we're ready. Maybe tomorrow. In the meantime, life is good here in the City of Rest, so it must not be the right time to proceed." Having finished this long speech, the young man took a good look at Traveler. He saw a bedraggled, shivering young woman.

"But listen to me babbling on. How rude. Please take this coat. It will keep you warm."

Traveler put on the coat. Immediately she felt warm and secure. She knew she wouldn't want to leave this place, whatever it was, any time soon. The city was pleasing in a bland sort of way. Two brick streets intersected at a small park. The City of Rest had no particular beauty, no endless sky or sweeping vista like Long Look Mountain. It had no outstanding architecture, nothing to take her breath away. Yet, there was a certain something, perhaps the thatch-roofed cottages, that made Traveler feel safe.

The front yards of the cottages were neat and tidy, with shrubbery and lawns. One bush, which grew in most of them, looked familiar to Traveler, much like the Berry of Deception Bush. She was quite sure it couldn't be. Who would let that detestable bush grow in their front yard?

Traveler waved to a woman working in front of a cottage. The woman waved back, distractedly, for she was busy following a tangled vine to its end. Traveler felt a tinge of uneasiness. That couldn't be the vine that grew from the Seeds of Curiosity, could it?

The young man spoke again, "Would you like me to show you around?" He smiled.

"Why, thank you," said Traveler, forgetting all about the woman and the vine, "that's very kind of you."

As they walked the streets of the City of Rest, Traveler noticed that all the people wore a coat very much like hers. "Why, I fit right in here," she thought. "I must belong."

The young man pointed out various sites as they walked. "There's the Spa of Respite," he said. "Sometimes when I get to feeling anxious, like maybe I should move on, I go over and sit in the waters. Then I calm down. And over there, that's the Bide a Bit Inn. I try not to go over there. Seems the people who stay there don't stay here too long. We can find you a place to stay later."

"How nice of you." Traveler was taken with this new friend.

A woman about Traveler's age stopped them in the middle of the block. "Hi," she gave a big friendly smile. "You're new, aren't you?"

"Yes," Traveler replied, "and sorely in need of a rest."

"You look it," the woman replied. "I'm on my way to a party at the Statue of Recuperation. See over there in the park? Why don't you join me?"

"That sounds like a perfect way to unwind from my journey," Traveler responded. She gave a brief thought to letting Companion know where she'd be. But he was nowhere in sight. Well, it was a small city, and she felt quite sure she couldn't get lost here. He must be near.

Sandi Patti

Traveler joined the group of Voluntary Passengers who were holding hands while singing and dancing around the Statue of Recuperation. After a while, growing tired of the party, she decided on her own to go back to the Bide a Bit Inn.

That first night she slept dreamlessly, awoke refreshed, and joined the Voluntary Passengers for yet another party. And that day passed, and another, and another. Traveler was growing used to feeling content. "Maybe these people are right," she thought. "What reason is there to go on searching for the Homeplace, a place I've never seen, when this city is so peaceful?"

Traveler was walking down the brick path when she had this thought. Suddenly she tripped and almost fell to the ground, sending her mind instantly back to the Narrow Path. Where was it now? Something inside her whispered, "You've got to find it." Her heart said, "This isn't your home."

That little stumble brought Traveler to her senses. She realized that she hadn't even thought of Companion for days. How long had it been?

Her sore muscles had healed; she felt energized and refreshed from her long sleeps. She called out to Companion, "I miss you. Where are you?"

As always, he appeared by her side. "Here," he said. "Don't you think it's time we leave this place?"

"Oh no!" Traveler was stunned at her strong reaction to his mild suggestion. After all, just a minute ago she'd been longing for her path.

"Traveler," Companion was gentle, but persistent, "rest is good for you. In fact, the parties here bring happiness and laughter. But do they truly bring joy to your heart? You see, these former travelers, who call themselves Voluntary Passengers, have misinterpreted the reason this place exists. It was created to give pilgrims a place to rest on their journey and a taste of the joy to come. They've attributed the happiness in their hearts to the City of Rest itself, not to its Creator."

Traveler appeared to be listening, so Companion continued. "I want to tell you a story," he said, "about a time when I too was given an opportunity to stop at a false place. I was taken high up on a cliff

Sandi Patti

and told that all I saw could be mine to rule and take pleasure in—if only I'd stop traveling back to my Father—if only I'd deny him."

"And what happened?" Traveler asked. Companion had her full attention now.

"Why, I couldn't do it," Companion replied simply. "I could never give up my Father. I just knew in my heart I couldn't, no matter what came next."

"And did you go back to your Father?" Traveler asked.

"Yes," Companion replied thoughtfully, "yes, I did. And because I did, every pilgrim who wishes to do so also can go to my Father in the Homeplace. Let me show you the real joy at the end of your journey."

Traveler grinned. Then she began to chuckle. "Oh, Companion," she laughed at herself. "I don't know why I thought this was a good place to stay. To tell you the truth, I'm getting a little sick of parties."

Traveler realized she was enjoying a moment with her dear Companion and laughing at her own foibles was at least as much fun as a week of parties. And she knew in her heart it was time to move on.

Le Voyage

Traveler left her Coat of Complacency near the Statue of Recuperation. Singing with every step, she and Companion left the City of Rest.

VI

*T*RAVELER AND COMPANION passed many days walking the Narrow Path. Traveler felt so full of joy that she made a resolution. "Never again will I wander away from you," she stated emphatically to Companion.

He simply looked at her with great love in his eyes. She grew wiser under his gaze.

"Well, I've learned not to say 'never'," she amended. "But I do resolve that if I wander, I will not wait to call out to you for help."

Companion was well pleased with this resolve. "Now you know," he said, "that I will not judge you, or lecture you, or make you feel like a bad person. I love you without bounds."

"And I will stay with you because you love me and because I

Sandi Patti

want to. You truly are my Companion," Traveler replied, feeling well satisfied that her heart indeed had found a home, though she traveled still.

Soon after that, Traveler once again began to feel restless. The feeling started in the pit of her stomach and made its way to her throat, and finally to her consciousness.

"Companion, what is happening to me? I'm scared. I feel like something bad is about to happen. I know you are with me, yet I've never felt so alone, so frightened."

Traveler wanted to run away. But where? The fear came from inside her. Her eyes swept the terrain. Mysterious storm clouds were quickly filling the sky and there was an eerie sense of quiet in the air. Unsettling . . . An ominous silence much like sailors sense before a storm at sea. She knew she hadn't left the Narrow Path. It was here somewhere, even if she couldn't quite see it at the moment. To her left, a stream inched its way through crags in the rocks, met with a faster moving river, and dropped with fierce persistence into the lake below.

The waterfall might have been calming to Traveler, if it had not been entirely silent. She looked down into the water, expecting it to reflect her face or the landscape. But it didn't. It was too murky.

"Companion," she shouted, even though he was near and the quiet remained, "what is this place?"

"We are approaching the Forest of Fears, dear one," Companion replied. "I know you're afraid. If you have ever trusted me, trust me now. You are much closer to the Homeplace than you realize, but you must go through the Forest of Fears to reach it. There is no way around it. You must face what you fear most—yourself. I cannot face it *for* you, but I can face it *with* you."

"Oh, Companion, don't leave me!" Traveler didn't know how she could bear this.

"You can bear it, dear one." Once again Companion knew her heart. You have traveled far in answering your heart's beckoning. You have grown in wisdom and in strength as you have journeyed. You are strong enough to face the Forest of Fears. You must choose whether to do so. I cannot choose for you.

Sandi Patti

Traveler knew the choice she must make. She knew that if she did not go on she would never be content. She could no more go back now that she'd had a glimpse of Long Look Mountain, now that she'd felt Companion's love, than a butterfly can go back into its cocoon and become a caterpillar once more. She knew this in her heart, though she could not say it. So she simply said, "Companion, please come with me."

"Here, take my hand," was his answer, "and don't let go. I am with you always, as I said I would be."

Nevertheless, she felt paralyzed. Her feet felt rooted into the ground. But now she knew what to do. She called out to Companion, "Please help me put one foot in front of the other." And so they moved on, step by single step, until Traveler was striding forward, with some confidence in her steps. They headed down the rocky slope, right past the murky lake, and didn't stop once until Traveler spied an awful sight, right at the edge of the Forest of Fears.

A large, brown bush, branches growing off in all directions, contorted itself into shape after shape after shape. It never stayed still for a

Sandi Patti

minute. The branches groaned, creaked, and screeched, like they were in pain, as the bush shifted one way and then another. Traveler pointed her finger and whispered to Companion, "What is that grotesque thing?"

"Don't touch it," Companion warned Traveler.

"I have no intention of doing so," Traveler said, clinging even more tightly to his hand. "But what is it?"

"That is the Bush of False Security. It twists and shifts constantly, looking for a position that will bring it peace and happiness."

Traveler stopped staring at the bush and glanced at Companion. She paused, took one last look into the comfort of his eyes, and stepped purposefully into the heart of the forest. Intently studying her surroundings, she could just make out the shadows of trees through the heavy mist. Everything was familiar to her in a vague sort of way. It was as if her life passed before her eyes right there in the forest. Well, not her whole life, just the bad parts, the painful memories.

As if out of the very mist, she heard Companion whisper, "You've already survived the painful events of your past. You will survive the memory of them and face your fears. Hold on, Traveler. Do not let go."

And so she did, her fear of being unliked, her fear of not doing the right thing, and others, one by one. It didn't seem so bad at first. There was just enough light coming through the mist to help her see the path. Traveler felt almost in control.

Then, slipping deeper and deeper into the heart of the Forest of Fears, Traveler realized that nothing here was as it should be. The blackness choked her. Step by step, she crept forward, facing the fear of being alone, of not knowing her purpose in life.

The trees seemed to grow larger before her very eyes. The all too familiar bushes of the Berry of Deception loomed just off the path. Monstrous things with swinging limbs, they seemed to call out, mocking her. "You don't know truth. You wouldn't know truth if it hit you in the face."

In an effort to get her bearings, Traveler reached for her compass. She could just make out the gleaming needle, but it was no help. It spun round and round, making her dizzy.

Sandi Patti

Traveler knew then, for certain, that her compass was not her guide. She took a deep breath and forced her eyes ahead, searching for the path.

Standing right before her—had it been there a minute ago?—was the largest, most frightening tree Traveler had yet seen. Its mammoth trunk filled the entire path, butting right up against high rocks on either side. It grew tall into the mist, higher than Traveler could see. It had many branches and more than a few leaves, although this was no lovely summer tree. The brown leaves shivered, seeming to point accusingly at Traveler.

She didn't have to ask Companion the name of this tree. She knew the feelings it evoked all too well. This was the Tree of Guilt. And she saw no way around it. She could not climb the rocks it grew against. If she tried to climb the tree, she knew it would tangle her in its branches forever.

She no longer knew if Companion held her hand or not, for she could feel nothing. Her whole body was numb. She stood rooted to the spot.

Suddenly one of the limbs grabbed her leg. Traveler was desperate. She must do something. Crying out, "Companion, help me!" she flung herself directly toward the center of the large trunk and fell through to the other side, as if the tree were made of the very stuff of the mist around it.

Traveler felt, rather than heard, the huge tree fall behind her. She had faced her guilt, the guilt for all the things she had done to hurt herself and others, the guilt for all the things she hadn't done, and perhaps worst of all, the false guilt that made her feel like she was responsible for all the bad things in the world.

Slowly Traveler sat up. But the darkness hadn't lifted. She could still hardly see at all. The monster Tree of Guilt was gone, but her other fears were still there. She knew she had not yet left the forest. Her leg was scratched, she'd bumped her head, and most of all, her heart ached. Traveler had never been so tired.

"Where are you, Companion?" she barely had the strength to mutter.

In the silence, she felt the gentle hand on her shoulder and knew he was near. She tried to see the path, but it seemed to have

Sandi Patti

disappeared into the mist and the shadow of the trees. She tried to get up, but her legs wouldn't hold her.

"All right," she said to herself with more resolve than she felt, "if I can't walk, I will crawl." And crawl she did, on her hands and knees. She could hardly believe she was making progress. In the midst of the darkness, pain, and fear, she inched forward on her knees with Companion by her side. Yet, even this halting progress became more difficult. Traveler thrashed her arms about, trying to feel the path. It had disappeared. She tried to stand again, and could not.

She was about to scream her frustration when a voice inside her said, "Be still and wait." So she did. She had no idea what she waited for. She simply waited.

And then she felt a tug on her hand, so slight she almost missed it. Had she not been sitting so still, she would have missed it. Gently, ever so slowly, Companion pulled Traveler to her feet. Then she felt another tug. Companion was telling her the direction. He tugged and she took a step. She waited for the next tug and took the next step. Sometimes it seemed like hours between the tug and the step, but now she knew waiting patiently is also sometimes part of traveling.

> *All my effort fails me here . . . fails me now*
> *Only the power of God can rescue me from myself*
> *I'm a traveler in the forest of my fears.*
>
> from "Forest of Fears"

Traveler didn't know how long they progressed like this. But after a while, a brisk wind began to push her forward, faster now than she wanted to go. She had all she could do to keep her balance. The wind blew away the mist and Traveler could see before her a deep crevice that seemed to have no bottom. Its very emptiness exuded power, seemed to beckon her. With horror, Traveler realized she felt the urge to jump in. And she instinctively knew that this was the Pit of Temptation.

Without warning, the very rocks underneath her feet shifted up and she began to slide. Traveler grabbed for a rock, trying to hold herself back. Her fingers bled, and still she slid. Traveler flung herself to the ground,

Sandi Patti

trying to hug the rocks so she wouldn't slide in. The rocks slashed her body. She knew that if only she could hold on, the pit would close.

Images of times past when she'd tried to hold on by herself swept over Traveler like a cyclone of memories. Screams. Tears. Disappointments. Tragedies. Lost love. She realized that in her whole life she'd never been able to hold on by herself. Somehow, she'd always let go.

With her feet about to slide into the abyss, Traveler remembered Companion's words. "I cannot face it for you, but I can face it with you." Wanting to believe these words with all her soul, and longing for them to be true, Traveler released her grip. Just before she plunged, she reached out with her heart, not her hands, and clung, not to the rocky ground, but to Companion's words.

Abruptly she stopped her downward slide, and just as abruptly the pit of Temptation shuddered and closed. Traveler had found the secret to avoiding the pit, not her own strength of will, but her humble affirmation of faith and trust. Traveler wept tears of joy. Then, exhausted, she collapsed and slept.

Traveler's body claimed long overdue rest. When she awoke, she sat up slowly, feeling the aftermath of her struggle in every muscle, joint, and bone of her body. She looked down at herself, amazed by the array of scrapes, scratches, bruises, and blisters. Her clothes had been torn by the branches of many treacherous trees. She was a mess. And she did not yet know that she was no longer in the Forest of Fears.

"Companion, what has happened to me? I look like I've been in a battle."

Companion smiled lovingly. "Little one, you have indeed been in a battle. You had the courage to face the most terrifying part of your journey. I am so proud of you, Traveler. You are a brave one."

"Where are we now, Companion?" she finally became aware of her surroundings. "It's so peaceful and quiet."

"Look around you," was Companion's only answer.

Traveler saw that they were sitting in a field of grass on the top of a little hill beside the path. Looking ahead she could see a beautiful valley, so alive with color and beauty and yet so understated in its simplicity. It reminded her a bit of Long Look Mountain. And looking even farther ahead, to the other side of the valley, Traveler saw another mountain. Light came from the very top. Could it be that there was a city up there?

"Oh, Companion, everything looks so . . ." she fumbled for words, "so new, so alive. Tell me about this place. I want to know everything."

"You have walked through the Forest of Fears, Traveler. You faced the pain inside yourself. You willed yourself to look straight into the face of your fear."

"I remember that part," Traveler said with a shudder.

"But you did more than that. You were changed completely at the Pit of Temptation, for you learned that you cannot resist temptation by yourself. You cried out to me with your heart to be with you, and I was."

Traveler sat lost in thought for a minute. Then she reached for her pack. She drew out her beloved compass and gave it to Companion. "I think" she began slowly, "that I have been trying to find my own way with this compass, even when you've been here to guide me all along. You must take my will and make it yours."

Companion closed his hand around Traveler's and the proffered compass. "Yes, yes," he said. "You have learned your lesson well. I accept your compass and I return it to you freely. For I know that, having given it to me, you will make good use of it."

"As you say, so I will do," said Traveler, bowing her head.

"Now, little one," Companion said cheerfully, "didn't you say you wanted to know where you are?" Traveler nodded and he continued. "We are in a place called the Tenderlands. It is here that the Flower of Mercy blooms fragrant and the Tree of Compassion never ceases to bear fruit. Love grows here. Your tears flowed freely in the Forest of Fears, and while you struggled I gathered them all to water the Tenderlands. It is your tears, Traveler, as well as those of many others, that help give life here."

> *The world is pure where mercy lives*
> *This heart becomes the grace she gives*
> *Her gentle words I understand*
> *They rise as mist in the Tenderlands.*

from "In the Tenderlands"

Sandi Patti

As they began down the path through the Tenderlands, Traveler thought she smelled food. She didn't mention her hunger though. She didn't want to appear not to appreciate her surroundings.

Just then, Companion said, "I could sure use a bit of refreshment."

Traveler stopped and stared at Companion. Then she laughed, "You've done it again."

"What?" he asked innocently.

"You always have a way of sensing my need and expressing it without sounding like a know-it-all. And you got it right again. I'm famished. But where will we find food? There's no inn in sight."

Companion answered quietly, "My Father will provide."

"Is it my imagination, or are those people coming toward us?" Traveler's question reflected her excitement. Then remembering her tattered clothes and bruised body, she became self-conscious. It didn't seem to matter how worn she looked to Companion, but what would these people think of her?

She quite expected these newfound pilgrims to reject her once they got a good look at her wounds. So she was more than a little surprised when they not only didn't turn away, but greeted her and offered bandages, soothing balms, new clothes, food, drink—everything Traveler needed.

It was as if these new unexpected friends had been anticipating her arrival. Some called out friendly greetings to Companion. Others didn't know him, but responded warmly when they were introduced.

Traveler thought she recognized a couple of the people from earlier in her journey. In fact, one of them strongly resembled Challenger, although his features were softer and he looked older. "How did *he* get here?" she wondered. "The last time I saw him he was goading anyone within earshot. And he wasn't very nice to me either. How could he have come this far along the path?" She felt quite irritated and, well yes, betrayed.

Companion, as always, was listening to Traveler's heart. "I said to you long ago, my dear, that each one must choose the direction of her own journey. You cannot walk another's path. It is not important how Challenger got here. He is here. And, for this moment, once again your path and his have crossed. He has as much to offer as do these other friends. They know pain. They too have been wounded in the Forest of Fears. Let them help you soothe your wounds. Receive freely from them, Traveler," he stopped for a breath. "And now, let's eat."

And so they did, as soon as Challenger and the others had bound up Traveler's wounds and helped her into her new clothes. Traveler knew that Companion spoke the truth, and she felt her heart soften toward Challenger. It no longer mattered to her that things didn't make sense. She was able to tenderly receive the gifts of mercy being lavished upon her.

> *With some unexpected friends*
> *Never asking where I've been*
> *Just a hand of mercy and words of love*
> *Call me back again*
> *Oh, it feels like home with unexpected friends.*
>
> from "Unexpected Friends"

After they had all eaten and spent time sharing their stories, Traveler got some well-earned rest. As she was drifting off to sleep, she reflected on her new friends and the lessons she'd learned here in the Tenderlands with them. To recognize and meet others' needs, to show them love and compassion, is essential to any traveler's journey. But it is also essential to allow other pilgrims to recognize and meet your own needs. "There's a time for both," she murmured to herself just before she fell asleep. Love truly did grow in the Tenderlands and now in Traveler's heart as well.

Traveler and Companion spent some time in the Tenderlands, greeting new pilgrims, binding up wounds, feasting together. But soon, too soon Traveler thought, came the day when she knew she must move on. She yearned to stay just a little longer, to tell her friends how they had strengthened her, renewed her, and made her feel special. But at their actual parting, words failed her. All she could say was, "Thank you, thank you . . . for everything. I will never forget you." And she hugged each one with a tenderness and love she had not known until her recent experience in the Tenderlands.

Many tears fell as they hugged. Companion felt it, too, the bittersweet portion of love. It is good to love and be loved in return. That

Sandi Patti

is the sweet. The bitter comes in the parting. Companion already knew what Traveler was now feeling. There is no sweet without the bitter, and no bitter without the sweet. That is the way of the journey, the way of preparing for Homeplace, where all that is bitter and all that is sweet are replaced with something far greater.

Following the path out of the valley of the Tenderlands, Companion and Traveler walked in silence for some time. Perhaps Traveler was instinctively gathering her resources for the last climb ahead.

After a time, Traveler began once again to notice the terrain around her. They had left the valley and begun to climb. There were sharp rocks by the side of the path. The vegetation was sparse, and the air hummed with the relentless buzz of small insects. The mountain cast a huge shadow over their path, chilling the air.

Even though the air was dank and dark in the shadow of the mountain, when Traveler looked up she could see the light glowing from the city above. She was closer now, and could make out a gate of some kind and see that the city was far larger than she had at first thought.

"Ah," she thought with a peaceful anticipation, "I am almost there. For surely that is Homeplace." She felt as if she could float up to the outer wall of the city.

"Yes," Companion responded to her unspoken thought, "there on that mountain is the place your heart has yearned for. It is within reach."

Overwhelmed, Traveler sat down beside the path to ponder her position. This is what she had longed for, what her journey was all about. She remembered back to the early days, when she thought she knew where she was going. She remembered leaving Familiar Trail, the road her family had traveled. She remembered meeting Challenger on the Road of New Beginnings and then leaving his group on the Road of Uncertainty. She thought too of the time she had started on the Road of Good Intentions.

She recalled the beauty of the Little Narrow Gate and Long Look Mountain. She remembered with some sadness the Voluntary Passengers in the City of Rest and wished they could see what she could see now, looking up to the top of the mountain. She shuddered when she remembered the Forest of Fears and the Pit of Temptation and then smiled when she recalled Companion's unselfish assistance in facing them with her. And last, she shed a small tear in remembrance of Challenger and the others in the Tenderlands. She surely hoped to meet them again in the Homeplace. Yes, here she was, finally, all of her experiences having brought her to the very foot of the Homeplace.

Companion spoke softly, "It is good, dear Traveler, that you remember these things. Your tender heart will serve you well, but only if you combine it with the guidance from the Homeplace. From now on, always keep your ears open to its leading, your eyes open to its vision, and your arms and legs willing to do its bidding."

Traveler nodded to say that she thought she understood. And Companion continued, "At this moment you are still not at the Homeplace. You have traveled well, but like each and every pilgrim on this voyage, you must use your newfound strength to traverse your Own Last Great Mountain. No two mountains are alike, and yours has not been climbed by any other pilgrim. Rely on your heart to guide you.

When you are so tired that you feel you have reached the end and cannot go on, remember this moment when we sat in peace."

Companion's words encouraged Traveler, and she felt ready to proceed. She studied the path, which wound its way to a cliff and there seemed—could it be so?—to proceed straight up. Trees actually grew out of that perpendicular rock, making it appear as if the land around them had been turned on its side. Traveler gulped. "Is this the only way?"

Companion nodded, a comforting nod. And Traveler began up the path, to the place where the cliff rose. Step after step, grip after grip, she ascended. As she climbed, the sky grew overcast, and a thick mist once again surrounded her. Was Companion with her, as he said he would always be? She took strength from the thought that he was near, even though she could neither see nor hear him.

At times, she felt like she was going backward, not up, so steep was the angle of the path. Yet up she went, upward, upward, upward.

Her muscles screamed for release. Her fingers grew numb. She began to doubt she had found the right path. "Try, try," she screamed

Sandi Patti

aloud to herself. Yet she could barely hear herself over the incessant wind, which blew just as hard as it had in the Forest of Fears. It seemed intent on keeping her from reaching the pinnacle.

She gripped the Branches of Perseverance, which grew out of the side of the mountain, and held on for dear life as she pulled herself up. As she rose higher, the branches came fewer and farther between. Only halfway up the mountain at this point, Traveler saw no way her endurance would last long enough for her to reach the top. She saw no place to rest, and her grip was slipping.

The wind grew ever stronger, rising to such a pitch she couldn't even hear herself think, let alone talk. It took all her resolve just to hang on, never mind climbing. But climb she must, and so she did, hand over hand, finding tiny toeholds as she went.

And she might have succeeded in her frontal assault on her Own Last Mountain, too, had it not been for one spiny, small creature. She reached into a crevice, bound to drag herself up farther this time, and *snap!* It stung her. With a scream of shock, she lost her grip and fell

Sandi Patti

one last time, backward down the mountain, her body battered by the jagged rocks, rolling over and over, until she landed at last, fifty feet below. Spinning in incredible pain, fear, and surprise, Traveler lay there. She tried to open her eyes, but the fear of what she might see kept them shut. "Companion, Companion, have you forsaken me?"

> *Down my own Way of Sorrows I carry my cross*
> *On a journey that's just as He planned*
> *Bearing scars of my Master's*
> *My heart's near His own*
> *I may die by myself . . . but I'm never alone.*
>
> from "No Place to Lay My Head"

"Open your eyes, Traveler," his voice came from nearby. And open them she did to the most amazing sight of her long journey. Where she had fallen, a path had been carved out of the rock. And beside it was another path, carved even more deeply into the rock.

"How can this be?" Traveler asked herself. "I seem to have made a path by falling. But where did the other path come from? Companion told me that no other pilgrim had climbed this particular mountain."

"I have gone before you," came Companion's reply to her unspoken question.

The realization hit Traveler with great power. Companion had actually gone before her on her Own Last Great Mountain. Not only was he always with her, but he had experienced every last thing she had. The same pain and suffering, the frequent wondering, the tired mind, the aching muscles, the tears of hurt, even the Pit of Temptation. Traveler finally saw that this was a relationship that knew no bounds of time, place, or circumstance. He was a tower of strength, a giver of life, her Companion.

"He has done it, but can I?" Traveler asked herself. She doubted she could go on, even on the newly made path. And that's when she remembered Companion's words: "When you are so tired that you feel you have reached the end and cannot continue, remember this moment."

Sandi Patti

As traveler remembered, she found strength to go on.

She arose. She placed her hand on the new path, and began to climb. The ascent went quickly. Steps appeared in the rock wherever she needed them. Soon Traveler reached the summit, and with one last pull found herself once again kneeling at the feet of Companion.

"Welcome, dear Traveler, to Homeplace. I bring you love and I wish you peace."

Homeplace, the ultimate destination of Le Voyage, reached at last. Traveler, Seeker of Truth, had found the Ultimate Truth. Now nothing else mattered.

Traveler raised her head slowly to the quintessence of beauty around her. A golden hue bathed the whole place in light, the likes of which she'd never seen. And there was music—elegant, joyful music, such as her ears had never heard. Giant pillars of alabaster stood at an entrance some little way off.

However, the majesty of her surroundings was no match for the love shining in Companion's eyes. Traveler felt stronger and more joyful under his gaze than she ever had before. Slowly, she rose and took his hand.

As they walked forward on the new path, now alive with color and beauty, they came once again upon the Little Narrow Gate, its door still resting open. This time, however, it led directly to the Homeplace and new life. How precious it looked. With one last deep breath and a gentle squeeze of Companion's hand, Traveler walked through. Behind them, an Unseen Hand quietly closed the gate.

As they came closer to the pillars at the main gate, Traveler could read the sign mounted on the main entrance. It read simply, "Vive Le Voyage."

The Journey Lives On!

We are all travelers, of course—in one way or another—travelers in this land called life. The adventure of the journey comes not just from reaching the ultimate end, but also from the traveling itself, the pilgrimage, the journey, "Le Voyage."

None of us knows where our journey will lead, or when it will end. None of us knows what the Homeplace will look like. All we know, and all we need to know, is that we have a faithful Companion to lead us there. Homeplace truly does exist. And in it, a place waits for each of us, fellow Traveler—

I have always loved stories. I love to hear them, read them, watch them, and tell them. Although I began writing this book through the eyes of Traveler, it quickly became my own story. My hope and heart's desire is that you will also see yourself. The journey is as much or as little as you want it to be—know that your Companion and the Homeplace are always waiting for you.

Sandi Patti